Dead Man's Mayhem

I0623180

Cyan Deane

author of Execution's Karma

Dead Man's Mayhem

DEAD MAN'S MAYHEM

Copyright 2012 Akirim Press, Cyan Deane
An Akirim Press publishing
Book Cover Graphic Design by Mirika Mayo
Cornelius at Akirim Press/ akirimpress.com

ACKNOWLEDGEMENTS

Thank God in Heaven, His Son and Holy Ghost.
Thanks to the living loved ones and those who have
gone before me. Thanks to the readers who go on to
spread the word about this book from every angle.

Cyan Deane

Life on earth after death can be a trip sometimes.

Dead Man's Mayhem

<u>Table of Contents</u>

Dead Man's Mayhem

Dead Man's Mayhem

Technically, things are bad for me now. Everyone thinks I'm dead. Yeah, I wish I was dead, but due to my completely ill fate, I'm totally brain alive with everyone making arrangements for my funeral. Pretty fucked up being in this state, having been lying in my coffin for approximately five hours since I started guessing the time, and not one single limb of mine is working enough to even wiggle a pinky toe.

The only reason I'm alive right now is that my ass was scared to even die, so much so that in my will that I made at the age of twenty-one, I exercised my right to no embalming, cutting, or autopsies to be performed on my body when I kick the bucket because of this very thing – I might still be alive. Sure enough, I'm here at the age of thirty-two with a shit load of anxiety to prove it while lying in a coffin.

In my will, I asked to be wrapped up, like a mummy with only my head showing for my funeral services, and now that I'm here for the viewing, I want to take the time to say that this shit sucks. I'm fucking hot as hell, and then they have my bottom half encapsulated in this coffin while this hot ass suit covers all the damn mummy wrap. Thank God it's cold in this area or I would have died from damn heat exhaustion by now just in time for the dirt to hit the wood.

What pains me even worse is that I'm waiting for people to arrive to simply look at my corpse. What kind of madness is this, anyway? Like, who does that? Planning their whole fucking day around a damn dead person. At least in my case, it's different. The people coming to see me lie in this forsaken padded box are going to end up seeing me alive, yet appearing dead. I hope I'm able to lunge out of this hell with handles before the burial.

"Well look at him, Jenny. He didn't look this good when he was alive and walking around us every week! I tell you, time sure does fly when you know you have to die, doesn't it? No matter how good he looks lying in this ole box, word is that it was something big that took him out of here besides that hit on the head."

"What's that you talking, Mary? They say Clive was a decent man. He may have had his share of ups and downs just like everyone else, but he was getting on the right footing each and everyday he was alive, minus the day he was knocked. He lost his footing that day, but every other day from, what I know about him, was pretty normal and decent."

"You think that because you don't know the people that I know that know about him, Jenny. Live long enough. You'll hear the talk, too. Goodnight, Clive, and may you rest in peace."

What the hell was that? If they don't get their little southern asses out of my viewing! Rest in peace? Mary made my life a living, breathing, stinking hell, and she has her sweaty panties coming in here trying to start some real shit while I'm still trying to wake myself up from this doomsday nightmare.

Mary – she's the lady that built the straw house that I wanted to crap on each and everyday to make that thing fall down right on top of her ass. When I would walk into her bar, for some reason or another, she would always be there. What owner is always at their establishment? That's the purpose of hiring people to work for you while you sit your ass at home and play golf in the middle of lunch time traffic so everyone can see what a grand life you have. She would make her baggy eyeballs twitch at me, and she's only forty one years old, looking and sounding like a grandma of eight hell raisers.

Truth be told, Mary would constantly talk shit, but it was shit that I could never hear. Call me paranoid, but she was ten words from getting popped in her mouth the day I supposedly went cold. I still don't even know who knocked me over my damn head in her nasty ass bar, but I swear it was probably her ass that set me up. She hated me, and I could tell. Her raggedy bar wasn't even that good for anything, but I was determined to go inside each and every week to make her life-long dream of store ownership reek of irritation with my presence.

I'd come to find out that I dated Mary's second cousin, Barbara Sue, back in the day for like three minutes tops, and Barbara Sue had gone and told her whole felon ass family that I was the one who broke her heart into pieces. First off, what they didn't know was that I would have never dated anyone seriously named Barbara Sue. Let's get that out there right now. Secondly, all I did was kiss her after talking on the phone with her for about one week.

When I met up with her, Barbara Sue wasn't really my type, but hell, the date was still on. We went to see a movie, parked it at the park, kissed and I took her snaggle toothed mouth home. It's true I never called again, but it was a damn shame how she ran my name in the mud about it. Obviously, Mary and her gang are still hating me for it, and this was made obvious by her smart remarks as I lay helpless in my coffin. Talking about I died of something other than a knock on my head. What the hell was she getting at? I'm as clean as a bar of soap on the side of a sink. My question is, who the heck hit me and why?

What was that? Oh snap, I can feel! Someone is touching me! Help! Open your eyes, Clive, open your eyes. Just concentrate.

"He looks good, and he hasn't changed color too fast being that he just died yesterday morning. I don't know why Clive always wanted the funeral to go so fast, but he used to tell me in college like this "*Dude, there are two problems with death. The first one is that it comes too soon, and the second one is they let people stab holes in you after the fact!*" He always said he didn't want that going down with him, and look at him now – all wrapped up with nowhere to go."

"Man, look though. We had some good times, me and Clive. It was just this week he was driving down the road, coming from his corner where he was selling his artwork. One thing is for sure, Clive, had a mad hand when it came to that paintbrush. Hey, David, I ever told you he painted my sister and her man getting married at the altar during the ceremony. Paid him a good grip for it, too."

"No kiddin', Tony?"

"No kiddin', man. Real talk. He was gifted. I'ma miss him. I'ma miss you, man. Rest in peace."

There it is again. He just touched me! Tony just touched me! Come on, self, lift at least one finger, just one, to let them know that I'm not dead yet. Look, Tony, look down at my fingers. No wait, wait! Don't leave, guys!

Bullshit. Just plain… I can't do this. Somebody has to wake me up. These dumb as hell morticians hadn't even checked on me, and aren't they supposed to be the pros? Can't they tell if someone is dead or not? I can't die like this. I'm about to be buried alive, man. Alive!

Where's my mom? She has to be able to tell if I'm living or dead. Hell, she's the one that gave birth to me, knows my scent, my expressions and everything about me. Yeah, when mom comes she will…

17

"Oh God! Oh, Lord, no, Jesus! My nephew!"

Auntie Bell? Did she just hit the floor? Oh no. I need to get up. Auntie, I'm not dead! Please, stop crying because I'm not dead.

"Get her up, Tommy, help me get her up. Mom, it's gonna be okay. Tell her, Tommy. Tell her it's gonna be okay."

"Mom, it's going to be alright. Please stop crying, mom, and you have to get up from this floor. Stop fighting against us, mom, and just get up. Put your arms around us mom, come on. You can do it. Breathe."

"Babies, you boys don't understand. I practically raised that boy, him and his brother, from the time he was born until five years old when he went to school. This shouldn't have happened to Clive, not Clive. He was such a good boy to me. Just like you boys. You all were raised together in the younger parts of your life. Tommy, you and Clive were like brothers at one point, you know?"

"I know, ma, I know."

"And Jonathan, you used to watch over them real good when they were out and about most times. What happened to you three? You used to be so close, it just hurts me to my heart to see this happening to my sister's child. It just hurts!"

"Ma, we just grew up and grew apart, but we love Clive, don't we, Jonathan? Always have and always will. Clive knows that. He's got to know that, ma, he's got to!"

Oh no, not Tommy crying, too. I know you guys love me, and I always have known that. It was my fault that things went sour with us for so long, but

I've always loved you guys. I just didn't say it in time is all. Tommy, don't cry, man. You were the better artist all the way around, and I cheated you out of that prize because I knew the judge was crazy about me. Look, go in the floor of my house and the prize is still there mixed in with all my life savings. I never used the five grand I won because I knew the truth. You can have it. I'm so sorry, Tommy.

And you, Jonathan. Man, you were just caught in the middle. I can't blame you for going with your brother, man, because he was right. I was wrong. It was all me. At first it was a joke, and I didn't know it would get to this point. My pride kept me from fessin' up. As a matter of fact, I never knew I would be classified as dead before I was able to give your brother the money. I fucked up, but please forgive my fuck ups, guys. Please. Don't go, guys, please don't go!

What's the point? No one can hear me. All my apologies are going down the drain. What drain? My bad. All my apologies are going down in the grave right along with me if I don't get out of here. I honestly can't see myself buried alive. That is fucking insane, and I'm not about to be the damn test subject for a bunch of maggots. Wait, what the hell is that smell?

"Clive, baby, it's me, Candice."

Well, Candice, your breath stinks! What's roasting in the back of your mouth that smells like a damn dead corpse? It ain't me, I know. Hell, I'm not anywhere near dead. My body's just still is all, but I really need to grow a slit to shut my nostrils from your bad ass, hollering breath, girl, damn! Move! Move! Shoot, kill me. Kill me right now if this girl doesn't back up about six paces and turn her back to me.

"Clive, you know it's been a minute, and I know I'm a little bit late plus coming through the back door and all, but I wanted to put something in your pocket, or just slide something under your hand, that I wanted to tell you. Since I'm here by myself, I'll read this letter really fast, and I hope you understand."

Just what the hell is this? Who the hell reads notes to a man that is supposed to be dead? I certainly hope this letter is short because, Candice, your breath surely isn't short at all. It's long and hanging and dragging up my nose, so read fast.

"Here goes…wait. Excuse me, I'm sorry, may I have a minute please in complete privacy. I'm sorry, it will be a short minute, thanks!"

Somebody come get this crazy ass girl who I barely damn know. Don't leave, whoever she's talking to! Grab her ridiculous ass and drag her out of here immediately, and take her to the damn dentist to get her tongue cleansed.

"Dear Clive. I need to whisper a bit closer to you because I really need to get this out so that I can clear the air, let the dust settle and move on with my life."

Why is it that the people with the smelliest ass breath got so much shit to say that actually smells like shit? Let the dust settle? More like let the mouthwash settle on those germy gums. It amazes me how people can't smell their own rotten breath. I mean, the air is inside you and when it comes out, how on earth does it manage to bypass the nose without coming back to slap the snot out of it? My whole theory about…wait what? What did you just say, Candice? Back up! Back up!

"…and when I told him to go into the bar, I knew that he would find you there. Thing is, I just didn't know that he would kill you for real, so I want to apologize for sending a complete stranger to me inside the bar because I really didn't know that he would do you any harm. I can't go to the cops about it because I was too stoned to remember what he looked like, but I do know that I was the one who told him you were in there…"

Stop crying and repeat what the hell you just said! You sent someone inside the bar to find me, and that dumb ass nearly killed me! Is that why I'm in this damn coffin?

"…but I will make it right somehow, Clive, I will. Keep this letter in the palm of your hand, and always remember that I'm so sorry for everything."

Get the fuck outta here! Some stink breath girl named Candice that I barely even know except for a hi and a tap on the butt with my right hand got my ass murdered, and she's too stoned to tell the difference between a funeral home and a police station. Heart please beat faster than what you're doing now because obviously I have an enemy out here that I didn't even know about, and I have to beat his ass.

Oh gosh no, don't kiss me, Candice, your breath! Damn, she did it! I can't even shake my head. Furthermore, I can't believe I was murdered, well, almost murdered, and Candice tells me everything in a dumb letter that she pushed underneath the palms of my hands. The fuck? I can't read it, Candice, and I missed half the story because I wasn't paying your stoned out ass any attention.

This is just my luck. Really. Of all the people who could tell me something, it's the stoner. Just great. And she actually writes. Wonderful.

Could someone just get me a police officer and a doctor, please? That would really be helpful at this point. You guys can't be serious about burying me alive. Sure my eyes are closed but … okay, Clive, get up. Stop waiting for people to help you and help yourself. Mind over matter, and right now, that's exactly what it isn't because the matter isn't doing one useful thing.

Before dad died, he taught me about concentrating on your body so hard that you can control everything about it. Some people can even stop their hunger, eliminate tension and all that, so now, Clive, let's see if we can get us up out of this coffin. Think…

"Hello? Oh hi! Call me back though because I'm at a viewing, looking over Clive before they drop him six feet down into maggots, worms and dirt. That's exactly why I'm being cremated because that shit is nasty! If I don't have organisms crawling all over me while I'm alive, then death isn't going to make it okay either. Burn my ass! Ha! I'll call you back though, Reese."

I forgot about that. How the hell long does it take for maggots to start eating away at me down there? What if I don't die until those nasty mother fuckers start crawling up my nose? I can't have ants, maggots and beetles laying eggs in my ears and camping out in my nasal passages…oh hell no!

Trina, wake me up. Tickle me like you used to tickle me when we hung out back in the day. You know, I'm ticklish, so go at it! Do anything to get me out of this stupor. How the hell is my central nervous system alive and my whole entire body is dead is beyond me, but…

"Rest in peace, Clive. We had some good times, and I hope they find the bastard that took your life. I still have that portrait you painted of me in the nude. My fianceé loves it even though we were being fast that night you painted it. He doesn't have to know that!. I didn't tell anyone, but I'm getting married next year, so even though you won't be there physically, your spirit is invited. I'll leave an empty chair just for you. Misses and kisses"

Oh Trina, Trina, Trina. I love me some you. My closest girlfriend next to my future wife…wait! Where is my fiancée? Why isn't she here right now? Does she even know I'm supposedly dead? She has to know because my mom would have called her up no matter where she is to let her know.

Calm down, Clive. Do your thing that you were doing before Trina interrupted. Get your body moving, and when mom comes along with Fee Fee, they will be able to see that life is still inside of me, wake me up and I can leave this joint. Set up some interviews with television stations about the guy who was almost buried alive.

Better yet, I could find out who it was who caught me off guard while in the bathroom at Mary's bar. The last thing I remember is that I was flicking Mary off as she stood next to the flat screen hanging on the wall. I chuckled and slid into the bathroom. I literally slid because there was some drink on the floor at the door of the bathroom. Then, I recall hawking up some back wash from my mouth, spitting on the floor where I slid because I was pissed that Mary actually saw me nearly break my ass, and then, I went to the urinal.

I'd put about three beers into my belly, and that was always my limit. I was done, and it was already coming out hard at the urinal. Next thing you know, my head hit the wall after being hit from behind, and I went out. I do remember grabbing the wall, but the most I did was grab at old piss that went under my nails from off the walls as I dropped to the floor.

Now, I'm here – fucking alive with nowhere to go. Well, I'm trying to go. As far as I know, I have no enemies, so as to who hit me, that's up in the air. I don't have much for anyone to want to rob from me but my art. I refused to get a regular job because I meet people every day that pay me to put them in a place unlike ever before when I paint them on canvas. They pay me, and I roll on to the next corner the next week. I hit the suburbs, the schools, and then I hit the lower income level neighborhoods, so just about everyone knows my face if not my name. Signed Clive. I always sign Clive.

I'm gonna die. I don't even know the color of this casket, but I know I'm in it and gonna die. This is so fucked up that I can't even cry, but I can feel the damn tears on the inside. I wish somebody would just come knock this piece of crap coffin over so I could tumble out. More than likely nobody will…

"Don't forget to sign the book, Ms. Janet."

"I won't. Just taking my time, that's all, sweetheart. Will you help me, honey. At least I still have one of you left."

Mom! It's my mom! Mom, you have to know I'm alive when you see me. I can't look dead to you. There's no way.

"Yes, ma. I'm here. I'm here now. Not going anywhere. You still have me. Fee Fee, are you okay?"

"Yes, Cleve, I'm going to be okay. I just…"

"Alright, Fee Fee, don't go in yet if you can't. Pull yourself together first. That was your fiancé and that was my child and Cleve's twin brother. You two are all I have now, so we have to hold each other together."

"We know. You're all we have, Ms. Janet. I love Clive, and he didn't even get a chance to find out…"

"Don't cry, Fee Fee. At least he left us a child to be born, my first grandbaby."

What! What! Felicia's pregnant! My Fee Fee is having my baby! When did this happen? She didn't even tell me! When did you find out, Fee Fee, huh? Oh my gosh, I'm too ecstatic right now! I hope it's a little girl, but better yet, a boy to carry my name on. Yeah, that's it. If it's a boy, we'll name him

Clive Wright, and we can play ball together, do artwork, and man, I can't wait. Now if mom would just wake me up, I can be on my way. She knows me better than anyone, and she would always say she could tell when something was wrong with me. If this isn't classified as something wrong, I don't know what the hell is.

"Oh my baby, my beautiful baby boy. I love him so much. I love you, Clive. Half of my heart is gone now. Half of it's gone, and when I see your brother, at least I will always see you in him, how you would have grown old…and, Clive, you're a daddy, baby. You're gonna be a daddy."

"Here, ma, take some tissue."

"Thank you, baby. Oh Jesus, I never knew I would lose my son, my first born baby, before I left this earth. He was born at seven thirty six, and you were born at seven forty at night.

Cleve, you and Clive were inseparable up until about nineteen years old when you dropped out of college."

"Mom, don't bring that up again. We just had two different paths in life. We weren't going to do the same things all the time because we're twins, ma. He's an artist, and I'm not made for school and all."

"I know, Cleve, I'm just talking. I love you both, and I just didn't get a chance to see you two together much like old times."

"Thing is, mom, is that we had good times. Still did…even after I dropped out. We shared different things, stories and even hung out away from the house sometimes. We loved each other, mom. Always. We're twins. Don't beat yourself up over that because we're two separate people."

"Yes, Ms. Janet. Clive always spoke highly of Cleve. They were friends and brothers, all the way up until the end."

"I love you, son. I'll see you in heaven soon."

Ma, I love you, too. I've always loved you, and I feel your hand on my chest, mom. I'm crying on the inside because life is lying to you right now. I'm not dead, guys. I'm not dead. Mom, don't let them bury me like this. Cleve, just stay here and watch me in case you see signs of life. For some reason, I can think and hear you guys. I don't understand why, but I can! Help me! I'm fucking trapped inside my head!

"I'm going back outside, Cleve. I can't look at my son like this anymore. All my tears are gone now, and my soul is aching, baby. It's aching. I've cried all night. Just want his wishes granted for the burial."

"Fee Fee, stay here. I'll walk mom back to the car, okay?"

"Sure, Cleve. I'll be fine."

"Alright. Come on, ma."

Bye, ma. I'm gonna try to get out of here! You hear me, ma! I'm gonna try! Fee Fee, baby, I'm so sorry I'm not there for you and my unborn baby right now. I'm sorry that this is probably stressing you out, but don't worry, I'm not dead. Carry my baby to term and eat right because I'm getting out of this mummy wrap. I am. Give me some time. There's no way I'm being buried alive. I need to leave my artwork to my child. Leave it to my baby. I have to change my will. I can't die now, I just can't. Believe in me, Fee Fee, and stop crying.

"I loved you, Clive. With all my heart, I loved you. Why did you have to do that, baby, why?"

Huh? What are you talking about, Fee Fee? Why did I do what? What the hell do you think I did? I'm the one in the coffin, Fee Fee, so what the hell are you talking about?

"Hey, Fee Fee. Are you okay?"

"Yeah, Cleve, I'm fine."

"It's over. We did it. Wipe your face."

We did it? The hell? Did what?

"You think everything will turn out okay, Cleve?"

"Listen to me, Felicia. He had it coming. He deserved it. That's my brother, and even I knew that he'd pissed off so many people that it would be easy for someone to knock him off. No one will ever know that the child is ours, and soon, we will end up being together openly."

"I've never been a part of something like this before, Cleve. Sure, I fell in love with you, but I keep questioning why we had to take it this far – well you had to take it this far. Kill him, Cleve? I did care for him, too, you know. Was this really the only way for us to eventually be together?"

What the fuck? Did I just hear that? I can't believe it! I can't believe this pack of shitholes killed me or fuck…had me killed! Felicia! Felicia, when the hell did you start sleeping with Cleve? That's my twin brother, and you two fucking murderers are lying to my mom, got her crying her eyes out, and this shit…this shit…

"Yes, Fee Fee. Don't clam up on us now. Don't you love me?"

"I do."

"Well, let's just get him in the grave before some how this whole situation turns wrong, okay?"

"What do you mean, turns wrong, Cleve?"

"I mean, Mary put something in his food, drink or something. I don't know the details, but all I know is it worked, Fee Fee, it worked! She hated him, but I knew, just as well as everyone else, that Clive had scattered enemies around here because he never fell back."

"What do you mean, never fell back, Cleve? No man falls back all the time when confronted or threatened. He stood up for himself…"

"Quiet, Felicia. The bottom line is that Mary did what she said she would do for me, and I don't know what else she concocted to get him knocked over the head, but that was all on her, not me.

Now, he's dead. From now on we don't talk. Mom will be fine soon. All wounds heal. Your guilt will pass…just like your love for him did and went onto me. Survival of the fittest, and though it didn't seem like it, I was always the fittest."

Man, fuck you, Cleve! And Mary! Musty Mary that damn bar owner that was just talking shit over my coffin put some shit in my drink or food? Is that why I got knocked out so easily? Is that why she's spreading all that shit about me having something like a damn disease that took me outta here? Her ass set me up along with my damn brother and fiancée! I'm glad I flicked her ass off before I hit the floor in that bathroom. I've surrounded myself with a bunch of damn liars, losers and killers.

And stand down to people? What man does that, Cleve, but your ass? That's the reason we never got along.

You let so many people talk shit to you that you dropped out of school, and I was tired of standing up for your whimpy ass. But now you got balls enough to try and kill me because you wanted to be me with your jealous ass. Then you go and get my fiancée pregnant, and why she wants to even sleep with your losing ass is beyond me, just fuckin' blows my mind! Hell, I hope that baby ain't mine now for real. What's really messed up is that no matter what, the child will end up looking like me anyway because me and Cleve look damn alike!

I knew he was always jealous of me from the start. I could do everything that he couldn't do, and was that my fault? Hell no! Cleve was never satisfied with who he was because he was always comparing himself to me, and that's the truth. I compare myself to no man because I'm my own man. If anything, I compete with myself at all times. Cleve was just too ignorant to see that he was a master at shit that made no sense to me like puzzles and chess. Shit like that. As a matter of fact, that's how his reasoning ass got my ass in this coffin – thinking up shit while my ass was busy drawing up people kissing and shit on the side of the road.

I've never been the perfect thinker, just average, but I'll damn sure make others think twice if they mess with me. They can take that to the grave. Well…wrong choice of words there, but shit, it's the truth. Man, fuck you and you, Cleve and Felicia. I hope your baby comes out looking like the next man's. If I wasn't stiff in this coffin, I would knock the shit out of both of you and make you lay in it.

Who the hell hit me? Fuck! I need a cell phone. If I survive this, my will is definitely being rewritten to include a working cell phone. Oh screw me! I forgot about that note Candice left in my hand! If these plottin' ass people look at my hands too hard, they will end up going after Candice and probably try to have her killed too because she knows something. Or either Mary will hear about the letter and push some poison on her just like she did with me.

"I can't believe he's finally gone, Cleve."

"Yeah, he's gone. So long, bro. So long. Let's go, and put on your grief face, Felicia."

"You shouldn't have cheated on me, Clive. Cleve, let me know about the whole thing. He had my back more than you. I used to love you, but your brother's the better man to me."

"Let's go. That photo was worth a thousand words to attest to the type of man he was."

Cleve told you I cheated! Cleve!
Hell, he was with the chick's best
friend. We both were in on it! And you
took a picture of me, Cleve? Seriously?
Felicia, did your dumb ass ask him how
he got the picture? It's because he was
there with me, and had a good time, too!

Well, good. Leave. I can't wait to
see my mom again face to face, and
then call the law to throw Cleve and
Flee in prison with Mary and her ugly
ass face. The good part about it is that
they didn't see that note Candice left,
and that means that there is still
evidence of a plot to kill me. So far,
Mary, Cleve and Felicia were in on the
shit, but dummies never finish the job.
Morons.

Come to think of it, when this
poison wears off Mary gave me, I'm
waking up out of this daze and going to
beat some serious ass. I'm gonna need
my sleep because later, there will be

noses broken, lips split and heads hurt. I'll show them what a stand up man looks like coming out of the coffin. They'll probably drop dead at the sight of me.

Oh snap! I can move my toe! Look! Look, look, look, look! My pinky toe is moving to the side. I feel it! I'm doing it! Come on body move! Somebody get me out of this overpriced box that's going in the ground! Is this a damn joke?

Six Hours Pass

It's dark in here. I can't see anything but at least my eyes are open. I'm assuming those were coins holding my eyelids down. I don't know for sure, and really, I don't care. The fact is that I can move more than I've been able to since I've been in this coffin.

I can move my torso a good bit, and my arms are steady since I was able to maneuver that hot ass suit coat off and loosen up this tight ass cloth. It's just my legs! My legs are inching along way too slowly if I'm to get out of here before the next round of people show up to move what they think is my lifeless body into the hearse. I need to be able to walk! Here goes though. I'm about to drag my ass onto this floor, and I know this shit is gonna hurt like hell.

Rock slowly, Clive, rock really slowly and carefully, but wait. What if this damn coffin falls over on top of my weak ass? Then what? Every time I try to talk, my tongue goes the wrong way and only gives me a moan. It's like my vocal chords have had a full on stroke! I can't call for help at all, but then again, who would I call? Is security up here with all these dead bodies or what?

Instead of knocking myself and the coffin over, I decide to try to lift the other half of the coffin lid up so I can see how much my legs really might be able to move if given the freedom. They say when you let a caged animal out, they run wild. Well, my damn legs better run like a fucking escaped con on death row.

Even though I'm still sweating from not being completely out of this cloth, I manage to suck in some cool air from this cold funeral home, sit up completely straight and move my hands under the other half of the coffin to lift it up. This thing is heavy as dang boulders! Thank the heavens the lazy dude that left this place didn't close up my coffin all the way! If he was supposed to shut me up, I don't know. All I know, is he left me a great way to breathe and get out, at least halfway for now.

Come on, Clive, you can do it. Lift! Lift this mother and lift it until it comes off! I feel like my insides are going to explode, but finally, the lid lifts, and I lean over with the weight of my body to help push the damn thing completely open.

Now would you look at this shit? Just look at it. I don't have on any damn shoes! My feet are wrapped up in this damn thick tissue and nobody put me on any shoes with this suit! It's not like people can see them, but dang! Can I at least be fully dressed on the day of my doom? Let me get my behind out of this coffin. I don't care if I have to slither my ass out of the door, I'm going full steam ahead.

Just like I thought, my legs are moving as slow as molasses. Therefore, I used my arms again to lift them one at a time over the edge of the coffin while leaning my weight back the opposite direction. This doesn't seem like a very good damn idea because I felt like I was about to fall my ass backwards. That's why I decide to put my legs back in the coffin because I still felt that I was gonna get trapped underneath the damn thing when it falls with me to the floor.

Instead, I decide to scoot my butt onto the pillow inside the coffin with my arms so I can keep most of my body from underneath the coffin – not if – but when it tumbles over. It's not likely to fall the way that I'm going to bust my head anyway.

When my butt gets comfortable enough for me on the pillow, I try to spin around to face the wall, but that doesn't work out like I planned. Instead, my dumb ass falls backwards out of the coffin, and my back hits dead center on the hard fucking floor. That damn flat ass carpet didn't help the fall either. Dammit! If I can't move now it's because I broke my skinny ass spine!

Luckily, the coffin didn't fall over, but if that sucker had a mouth it would sure as hell be laughing right about now. As I stared around the room again like a pregnant lady in labor, legs wide open on my back, there was absolutely no easy way out. I had to start crawling. No one heard me fall, and for some reason, sound comes out of my mouth that makes no damn sense. When I need to talk, I can't talk. Isn't that some shit?

Since I see no immediate help, I start inching toward the entrance on my arms. My toes help me the most from behind because they have the most movement, so I use them to push. The more I use them, I hope the stronger they get.

The door seems ten million miles away, but I'm gonna make it. I have no choice seeing as half the people I know, including my twin brother, was in on my death. I'd love to see the look on their faces when they see me in the hot damn flesh. I start to move my elbows against the floor extra fast because I have to stop these crazy ass lunatics right now. As a matter of fact, where is a damn phone?

I stopped cold as my eyes zoomed in on that stupid lock way up high on the door. There is no way in life or death I could reach that right now, so I need to call someone to let them know that I'm alive in here. Every single phone except a cell has a cord, and it's my job to find it. What a better place than the front desk, and that's where I'm going.

As soon as I reach the front desk, I find every single fucking cord and yank all of them down. Good for me, the phone came too, along with the computer and keyboard, knocking me in my head in the process.

"Mmmmmm!" I groan, slamming my fist into the floor as hard as I could which wasn't hard at all. As I continue to try bending my legs, I get irritated then and just stop. I have to pull my pants down and unwrap this shit. As I start yanking, I can't get the strips up high enough to unravel, so I start opening drawers at the desk to find a pair of scissors. What desk is complete without scissors? Gonna cut my ass out and take these bitches with me just in case I need to gut a fool. Might try to take my ass out again.

Three o'clock in the morning reads the clock, and my mind is telling me that by six o'clock, I need to be out of here. Finding the scissors was easy as pie, and now, off comes the mummy wrap. No wonder why I could barely move my legs. My damn knees are wrapped up so tight I'm probably about to acquire damn near five blood clots! These are some stupid mother fuckers. Why the hell do you need this cloth this tight on a dead man? Fuck this. I'm definitely changing my will this week to loose ass mummy wrap and not damn tight ass mummy wrap. I'm shocked my lungs are expanding.

After getting my legs out, blood rushed through them like a fountain and I bend them for the first time fully. Hell yeah. Although slowly, I stand, being certain I hold on to every single thing in sight. Dead my ass. I got their dead. Something isn't right still, but I'm alive enough to get to the bottom of it. Dead ass people are cold as hell, so what the hell were they thinking?

As I now begin to sit up even better, bending my legs good and all that, the phone looks like a pot of gold.

I'm calling David, one of the people who sounded like he was genuinely cool with me while he was making comments over my dead, hot body.

My fingers walk over the numbers on this ancient phone like a zombie. They don't work as fast as normal, but at least they work! I need to practice my hello.

"Hello, hello," I cough out because my throat is dry as the desert. My tongue weighs a mountain, but my voice hasn't changed so unless David passes out, he's coming to save me.

"Hello?"

"Hello." That's all I could say. Fuck! And this dude is probably drunk as hell so…

"What's up? Who's this?"

"Mmm,"

"Hey, man, look, who is this before I hang up the phone? I don't play these dumb games, man."

"Clive," I say to him, but it came out like *Live*.

"Who?"

"It's Clive, C-C-Clive, David," I spit out the best way I possibly could, so hopefully he hears that it's me by the sound and not the slur of my voice.

"Oh shit! Oh shit!"

The phone hits the floor, not on my end, but on his end. David is in straight panic mode, so it takes me but a second to know that he recognizes this voice of mine loud and clear – from the grave. What he needs to do though is pick up his phone because I don't have that much time.

I hear the phone again with breathing on the other end, so I continue on my slow rant of begging him to come get me. "David, come get me," I try to enunciate as well as I can, but this fool drops the damn phone again.

"Fuck! It's Clive! Hey, hey man, hey come here. Shit, bring your ass here, Tony! Clive is on the mother fucking cell phone!"

Oh boy. I'm about to have David and Tony come rescue me, so this is about to go faster than what I thought! I'm too excited to get my ass outta here as soon as Tony proves to David's drunk ass that this isn't a dream. Tony is sober. He was always sober, just cautious as hell. Don't do this, don't do that, not yet, wait, slow down, turn right, back up and then spin – shit that makes him the designated driver at all times.

"Man, you must be really drunk to think you hear Clive on the other end of this phone," I hear Tony tell David in the background. "Where's the phone, man?"

"Right over there near my bed, Tony, and look, man, I know what I heard. I'm not that drunk. I only had two beers, and my ass is quitting today. Going to church on Sunday and finding a wife on Thursday."

"Man, shut up." I hear Tony fumble for the phone. "Talk to me. Who's this? My man Clive is resting in peace, so this isn't funny. Don't play like this."

"Tony, it's me, Clive. You came last night to see me." I speak slowly into the telephone with hopes that he won't drop the cell like David did.

There was only silence until Tony asked a solid question that he knows that only I would answer right.

"If this is Clive, tell me what happened on my first date."

"You shit all in your pants in the movie theater."

"Oh shit!"

There goes the phone again. This has got to be bad because Tony doesn't curse. On the flip, that means I can expect a car here in about five minutes to get me.

"Pick up the phone, Tony, man!"

"Man, David, you weren't lying! Wait, are we dead, too?"

"Heck no, Tony, man you drove back home, remember?"

"Slap me, then, D. Slap me and make a mark!"

"Here goes."

I hear a loud whap across Tony's face, and then comes the argument.

"Ouch man, shoot!"

"Don't say shoot now, Tony. Say shit because you said it when you heard Clive on the other end of that phone."

"My bad, my bad. Lord, forgive me. That was a slip up."

"Ain't no my bad. That was my last shit. Well, this one is because either Clive is alive or we're dead."

Guys, pick up the phone. Pick up the fucking phone. I glance up at the clock as the time says it's going on four a.m. Naturally, I'm anxious so they need to come before I get found out. Tony picks the phone back up.

"Clive is the really you, man? Are you alive? You still at the funeral home?"

"Yes, so come and get me. Put on a mask, too," I requested slowly, and Tony didn't answer. "I will be at the door to unlock it, but the alarm. Bring

David. When it goes off, carry me into the car and drive fast."

"Oh boy, oh boy, oh boy, oh boy!" Tony panics just like I knew he would.

There he goes doing that thing that he does when he is caught between a rock and a hard place. See, Tony is a good guy, and always has been. Breaking into somewhere and basically taking a dead man isn't up his alley. He would rather call the cops or the damn hospital, which is probably what he will ask me next, and then let them handle it. Thing is, I don't want any of these fools that had a hand in my death to know I'm not dead. They can all believe that my body was stolen, and when I surprise their dumb, donkey asses, somebody is liable to drop dead anyway in my place.

"Clive, how about I send…"

"No, just come. Now, before it's too late. Please, I'm alive." At that, I hang up the phone.

The glass door to the funeral home was about ten feet away from me, so my only objective was to sit beside it, wait until I see Tony and David hustle up to the door and then unlock it. I'm sure this place has a dumb security system on it, so they better make it a quick in and quickly get me the hell out of here to freedom.

. . . . .

"Man, what the fuck?"

"Just get him in the car, David! Shut up and get him in the car. I'm about to go to jail for this one. I can feel it!"

"How, Tony, huh? If anything, we need to file a big ass lawsuit on the damn funeral home for arranging his funeral tomorrow! Look at his eyes man. Does Clive look dead to you?"

"He did earlier!"

"Well he isn't, man, that's the point! All this other stuff is irrelevant, right, Clive?"

I don't feel like talking right now, but as they shove me head first into the backseat, slam the door and spin wheels to get miles away from the funeral home while the alarm system is going off, I feel the immediate urge to speak no matter how slurred.

"Thank you. I'm not dead. Take me to your apartment."

"Man, hell no! We're taking you to the damn hospital," David responds.

"No hospital," I struggled to speak, and final-fucking-ly Tony spoke up on my behalf.

"Man, can't you see that he can't talk much. Give the man a break. Let's take him back to your place, we chill, and then after his throat or whatever comes back, then we can figure out what to do next. Got it, D?"

"Why my place?"

At that, Tony stops the car in the middle of the road. It's pitch black outside, my back hurts like a mother fucker from falling my ass out of my coffin backwards and these dudes think I want to stop in the middle of the road and listen to them argue about where to take me while we just left the damn alarm going off at the funeral home. My ass was almost taken to the fuckin' graveyard, idiots! Take me any-damn-where, shit!

"Keep going," I slur while shaking my head.

"No, we're going to my place," Tony decides on the fly.

"Why your place then?" David asks.

"Because you hesitated."

"The fuck?"

"You hesitated, that's why. Everyone knows the hesitation is the mistake. You hesitate, you die or some other stuff goes wrong like with Clive." He stares back at me through the rear view mirror, and despite the big turn your ass around and drive that I want to give him, I just stare right back.

"You mean like he dies again?"

I watch as Tony agrees by nodding his head up and down.

"Oh hell no! Then we'll get popped for murder!"

"He's already dead to everyone, David! So how can you murder someone already dead, dummy? Just shut up! Can't you see he's back there struggling to live again. Turn on the music…classical. I hear babies like that."

"Babies?" David stares back at me from the passenger's seat, but fuck it. I'll let them have this dumb ass conversation with themselves. All I do is stare out the front windshield.

"Yes babies," Tony responds matter of factly.

"Clive ain't no baby."

"Well today he is," Tony states as he barrels onto the next street. As we all press our weight against the seat so we won't spill over onto windows because Tony is driving so damn ferociously, we finally pull into the drive-way of Tony's house. It's not too far from the funeral home, but at least it's away from the shithole.

"How long is he gonna be here, Tony?"

"I dunno. Ask him, don't ask me, man. I'm just the driver as the two of you always say. Clive, hey Clive?" he calls but I continue staring forward. Every single damn thing I heard while I was in the coffin is coming to a head, and I was about to burst…into fucking tears. I'm a grown ass man, and I'm crying for the first time over some shit that ain't worth a shit.

I turn my eyes up to look at Tony through the rear view mirror, and these punk ass tears come rolling out. Tony gets panic stricken, and then dives into the backseat from the front. What the hell?

"David! David, man, it's Clive, man! He's leaking, Jesus, he's leaking!"

"No! Nooo!" I yell as deeply as I can, but it's too late. David opens the back door, grabs me under my shoulders and yanks me out of the car. Before I know it, I'm hanging upside down while Tony is holding my legs up in the air, so my tears can fall back inside my eyes.

"Push them back in, D, push them back in!"

"I'm not touching that! That's fluid. Guide that shit! I don't know what that is. Blow!"

That's when David starts blowing in my face to get the damn tears to go back inside my eyes. What kind of dumb ass shit is this? And what the hell does David and his drunk ass think I have, a damn disease? Boy, I tell you what! All I had was a moment, and they turned it into a fucking nightmare.

As I stare at the sky thinking that I probably need to be there right now, I muster up more vocal strength to say, "Those are tears! I'm not leaking!"

The two stunned ones glance at each other for about five seconds while I'm literally hanging in the balance like a damn gorilla until finally they stand me up and drape my arms over their shoulders.

"Sorry, Clive. I mean, I thought that you were leaking some…or oozing from the eyes or something like that because no sound was coming out. Never seen you cry before, man, my bad," Tony apologizes as he helps me up the steps as David opens the front door with his keys.

When we get inside, these two wonderful friends of mine drop me on the couch.

"Fuck!" I manage to get that out as they both stare at each other again like some fucking fools. I swear to God, you would think these bastard ass friends of mine would know that I am at least thawing out and shit, but no! They continue to man handle me as if I'm a store bought rag doll. If I could sock both of them in their faces with my fists, I would do so point and damn blank.

"Man, don't throw him down like that?"

"Me?" Tony responds pointing at his chest and looking around the room like this isn't his damn house. "You tossed him down, too. How was I supposed to know that he wasn't going to bend his knees and squat, dang!"

"He probably forgot or something, man! His brain…lack of oxygen or some shit like that… fuck!" David yells as he squeezes his head between his hands.

Tony throws his hands in the air out of pure frustration of the matter and says, "If his brain was so messed up, how on the cement of this earth would he have remembered your phone number early this morning? Even I can't remember your phone number this early, dude!"

"Clive," David plops down next to me and takes me by the face, "Man, me and Tony…well just me… I was just popping bottles back at my apartment for you, reminiscing on good times, looking at our suits hanging up thinking about your damn funeral tomorrow, and now this shit! Say something like … what the fuck happened?"

David's eyes look like to big ass rutabagas and his mouth looks like a damn carved cantaloupe as he waits on me to respond to his depressing question. When he finds out what really happened to me, the shit is going to hit the fan, and fuckers are gonna want to call the cops. I've already run it through my brain though. No cops will be called until I get my say so in front of all those mother fuckers in a couple more hours before the funeral home breaks the news that my body is missing.

"I can't talk much now. Wait." Every time I move the muscles in my throat, a sharp pain moves up to my ears, almost like something is getting stuck in the middle of that damn thing. I don't know what because I haven't eaten a good fucking piece of anything since I don't remember…well back at Mary's, I guess. "Drink?"

"Yeah, man," David responds, kicking Tony in the leg at the same time. "You heard the man! Stop staring. This is your house. Drink! Drink!"

"Man, don't kick me, man!" Tony balls up his fists at David.

"Well then move! You see he's about to die!"

"David,"

"What?"

"Shut up." As Tony goes to grab me a bit to drink, I watch David's mouth begin to pour out words again about basically nothing. Honestly, I wish he would have been the one to go make me up something to drink, but just my damn luck again. Thankfully, Tony comes back right before David starts giving me this spill about loving me. That crap I don't want to hear. I'm too alive to hear that love talk from a dude. Wait until I'm really dead, partner.

"Here, Clive. I got it though, man. Hold back," Tony says as he helps me drink the water slowly. At first, I thought I would choke, but then, the water starts to go down great with my reflexes and soothe my dry throat. I'm home free. I'm alive! Now that my throat feels much better, it's time to plan my plot.

···Forty-nine Minutes Later···

"Don't tell me that shit, Clive."

I nod my head, agreeing with David's shock after I just finished telling him and Tony the full out story of what my ears heard while I was dead.

Tony is still in awe, and finally asks, "Are you sure you weren't in some messed up dreamland? I mean, you really did hear Fee Fee say she was carrying your brother's baby and him and Mary concocted some plan to get you killed, and your brother sold you out at the same time over some other woman you slept with while some crackhead sent the killer in there to you?"

I sit up and stare them both in the eyes. "And that's why I need you to take me to Felicia's house right now. Don't call her Fee Fee anymore either. Maybe Flee Flee, but not Fee Fee."

"Now, man?"

"Yes, Tony. Right now. Get your shit…whatever shit you need. We're going to Flee Flee's house."

"I'm not going to prison over some stuff like this, Clive."

All I do is stare back at Tony's ass. "Do you think I'm cocked and loaded just getting my ass up out of a coffin, huh, T? All I'm doing is going to fuck some shit up mentally, not with my hands either."

"Yeah," Tony says grabbing his keys, "Things will be pretty messed up after they see a dead man walking."

David agreed. "Hell, yeah," he continues holding out his hand for a high five for Tony.

Tony agrees, but with a "heck yeah!" instead of the hell. Even though I was ready to leave right then, it was the responsible thing for Tony to lead the prayer as he always does in stressful situations.

"Man, we have to pray. I feel like I need to thank God…you need to thank God for allowing you to live through all this, and then we need to ask Him to guide your thoughts and actions as you enter into this next phase of your life."

"True that, Tony." I bow my head and wait. David does as well. This was the ritual, but as my head is bowed, nothing happens. I quickly glance up at Tony, and his eyes are still on me.

Shrugging my shoulders, I ask, "What?" slightly irritated.

"Man, the last time, I didn't know that you were going to die, and I never asked you about your salvation or none of that. It's even partially my fault because I know how you are, but I shouldn't have let that stop me being that you're so bullheaded."

Even though my blood is about to boil, I remain damn calm and ask, "What do you need me to do, Tony, huh? Get saved?" I look over at David. "Newsflash. I am saved. Betcha didn't know that, did you? I resurrected, didn't I?"

"Oh snap, he did!" David shouts, covering his mouth with his hand.

"The resurrection didn't happen yet, Clive," Tony responds while shaking his head at David.

"Why do I have to be the bad guy?" I ask about to blow my fuse. "I am saved. I just don't act like it all the damn time!"

"See."

"See what?" Bust my ass, I'm angry now. "Because I curse like a mother fucker? Is that why you think I'm not saved?"

"Yeah. You're my boy and all that, but I have to tell you that sometimes you don't act like you even know Jesus at all."

"Well, what else besides my cussin'," I glance sharply back at him and then at David, "like a mother fucker tells you that I don't know the Lord above?"

No one speaks. There is complete damn ass silence in here, almost quieter than lying in that cushiony, cottony coffin.

"Well?" I take a seat slowly on the chair again. "What the hell makes me unsaved?"

"Not unsaved, Clive. Just...follow me here." As Tony starts to explain his theory in hopefully less than two minutes so we can go, I sit and fume. "You see a pumpkin, you don't see a peach. Same color, but one is fuzzy and small and the other one is used for Halloween. You have a nice fuzzy exterior like a peach, but if I carve you at a certain angle, witches would gladly use you as a centerpiece."

"Tony," I interrupt.

"Yep?"

"Shut the fuck up." I stand up. "I know I curse too damn much. I also know that I do a lot of severely fucked up shit that Jesus would not approve of. I also know that," I stare up to the ceiling, "I'm not technically saved. What you just said got me scared because I really could be dead, so I am willing to get saved right now so the next time I'm in a coffin, I won't wake up next to Satan in a sweat suit."

As my anger left, I start to thank God for letting me live. Truth be told, I never pray. I know my prayers, and mom would slap the mummy wrap off me if she knew, but I never take the time to talk to Jesus ever. Without Tony, I would be completely prayerless. Now it's the time, once and for all, to seal this deal. Change my life now so that after I confront these killer ass people, I can walk a bit better and talk a bit better in my life.

"Ready?" Tony asked.

"Yeah, what do I do?"

"I want to get saved, too, man. Don't leave me out. I might die tonight, too!" David says, already on his knees, hands folded and eyes shut.

"All you have to do is mean what you say and believe what you say when you confess that Jesus is Lord, and you want to live for Him and rely on Him for all things."

"That's it?" David and I both ask.

"Yeah, so do it," Tony says while waiting.

"Jesus, I'm sorry for everything I've done and still having a problem stopping, like my cussing. I won't spell everything out, but I do need to change and I'm starting with You, especially since You've given me this second chance. Please save me. I believe in You, that You are Lord."

"Me too, Jesus. Help me out, and Lord I will try my best to do what I'm supposed to do down here. Just don't let me die like Clive did. I want to live. Amen."

Tony and I shake our heads. Drunk and dizzy David.

"You have to be sober, David."

"Oh. My heart is sober, Tony. It is, man." He turns to face me. "What? I'm dead serious. I want to be saved."

"God only knows."

. . .

There she is, asleep in the bed, next to Cleve. Why she still leaves the key in the bush for me, I don't know. Oh, yes I do! It's for Cleve, not Clive! Cleve, the Cain of the family, and since everyone thinks I'm the Cain, they'll be right happy to know that I'm actually Abel! I even got saved today, the day of my resurrection!

"Bastard." I whisper with my fists as tight as a constipated fart about to unload. Looking around the room, I don't even see my photo hanging up anywhere! Instead, there's a freaking photo of those two in the same exact pose as the photo with me in it except Cleve is wearing different clothes!

I'm about to crawl in bed with these two stupid asses. That's what I'm going to do. Watch these big killing ass liars have double heart attacks. My own brother! My own flesh and egg! Identical to the hairs on my toes.

While looking at the clock and making certain that Tony and David remain silent in the front room, I come to grips with lying next to Flee Flee instead of swatting her musty ass. I walk over quietly and lie down on the other side of her. I even drape my arm around her stomach while her breasts are pressed up against ole Cleve. It was almost five forty five in the morning. Time to wake up to get ready for the funeral.

"Good morning, baby girl."

"Cleve, baby, it's early."

"I know," I whisper in her ear and pull her hair back away from her face. "I just want to look at you is all."

I watch her eyes come open and stare at the wrong man in front of her who is knocked the hell out with slob dripping from his lip like a damn rabid dog. My insides hurt so bad because I was about to explode into a hysterical rage as I watched her call him.

"Cleve?" she asked confused, so I helped her disoriented ass out a bit.

"Yes," I answered from behind.

"Shit!" Ole Flee Flee jumps her pregnant ass clear over Cleve screaming like I'm murdering her.

"No, not shit. Shit, it's Clive. That's more like it." I respond continuing to lie on the bed with a huge fucking smile on my face waiting on this bitch to drop dead. I won't even catch her either. Just let her sloppy ass hit the damn floor.

"What's wrong with you, baby?" Cleve asked with his eyes barely open as Flee Flee continues to scream her fake eyelashes off. She looks funny as hell, falling apart and shit.

"Question is, what the hell is wrong with you, bro?"

"Oh shit! Oh shit!"

Boom! Stupid Cleve rolls off the bed and hits the hard floor. I look up to the silent, in shock and shaking Flee

Flee on the wall. Somebody get me a damn swatter.

"Now now now now, Cleve and Flee Flee, what are you two doing sleeping butt ass naked in the same bed with a framed picture of you two hanging on the wall? That shit had to be taken before I died, huh? Kept that shit hidden, didn't you?"

Cleve pokes his head up from the floor with those marble ass eyes with spit and shit stuck to the side of his nasty ass mouth. I ought to kick his ass right now, but again, I'm waiting on him to drop dead, too. At least if he did drop dead, I could ship his ass to the hole they have planned for me.

"Just what the fuck are you doing here, Clive! The fuck…" he yells, grabbing his jeans off the back of the bed while banging his back up against the wall trying to yank them up his legs as fast as he could. Flee Flee isn't even talking again yet, and as far as hiding her naked self, she isn't doing that either because I guess she's a whore like that. She doesn't even give a flying fuck who sees her lounging around in nothing but skin.

I grab a pillow, not the slobby ass pillow that was under Cleve's mouth but a clean one, and shove it under my arm as I continued to talk. "The only reason I didn't kill you two mother fuckers is because my boy Tony talked me into thinking about Jesus right before I brought my ass in here. Now, don't think for one second that I won't fuck y'all up if you try to run because this smile shit that's on my mouth is just a good fucking look. Really, I'm fucked up on the inside, but since I'm saved now…" I watch as Flee Flee starts to move her eyebrows into a what the hell kind of look. "No really, I'm saved now, and I have Tony out there right now in your living room praying like the heavens for me not to rip your fucking nose off your smelly ass face."

"This has got to be a fucking dream, Cleve," she says to him in that wack ass voice.

"You're a dead man! You're dead!" Cleve screams, squeezing his head in between his hands.

"Frankly, fuck face and fuck facer," I address them both, "I'm not. I am a little horny and tired though but I see that you, Cleve, have snuggled up to my fianceé quite nicely leaving me no room." My eyes turn to Flee Flee. "Isn't that right, Flee Flee?"

"Stop, Clive, don't! Don't you dare flip this on me! You were seeing someone else behind my back!" Flee Flee buzzes.

"Are you talking about that picture Cleve showed you, you freaking idiot? Did you ask Cleve how he boosted me up to doing it, too? Your baby's daddy? As a matter of fact, he was with someone, too, and even paid the chick he was with! Oh yeah, I know, you're pregnant with your fucking fake ass. You told me everything while you went over that murder plot above my coffin! Come here, Flee."

She stands there like she doesn't even hear me, but her ass can hear me clearly. If she can fuck me over like this then she can hear me quite damn well. I look at her, standing there naked as hell like a painting – still.

Therefore, I stand up and take a deep breath. "Get your ass over here!" I yell as a loud as my lungs can tolerate, and as soon as I said it, she jumped her stupid ass over in front of me crying and shit.

"Shut your damn mouth." Her mouth starts to quiver really badly, and then I ask, "Just who the hell told you that Cleve was me? Who the hell told you to have a sexual relationship with my twin brother, Flee?"

"Why are you calling me Flee?" she asks, tears streaming down her face.

"Because you're dusty! If you weren't pregnant, I would knock your dusty face in!"

"I loved you, Clive, but you cheated on me with some…"

"Ahhh, shut up." I throw my hands in the air. "I loved you, too, all the way to the coffin until you fucked up and told me that you and him plotted my murder. Both of you talked about it while my ass was in the coffin!"

"Look, Clive, man I'm sorry. You're my brother, and it was really her idea…"

"Me? How dare you, Cleve!"

"Hell yeah it was you! After I showed you that picture, you said you could kill him."

"Fuck you, Cleve! Fuck you! You know I didn't mean to kill him! You got all in my head," she cries, but that shit sounds stale to my ears.

"Looks like he got in your head, your ass…and your stomach."

"It still might be yours, Clive."

"Too bad. I'm dead, baby. Oh well." My attention turns to Cleve. "Come here, Cleve."

As he walks over, I see myself, and I want to vomit. The only thing that differs about us is our attitude. He's not a stand up man. His punk ass blamed a woman for his shit. What type of bitch move is that?

I meet him, eye to eye. "Cleve, you always wished you were me." I can smell his wake up breath. Mine smells better on any given morning. Bet he was jealous of that, too. "How does it feel, man, huh? You can't even kill me right. You had Mary put some voodoo shit in my food, and her ass did it, too. Call her. Tell her to bring her stupid ass over here because you need her before the funeral. It's a desperate emergency." I hand him Tony's cell. "Call her."

"No."

I hit his dumb ass upside the head with the phone.

"Call."

"Shit, man." He starts to dial. When she answers, I listen on the phone as she agrees to come immediately. Everyone else should be there because the funeral home surely won't be pulling up yet with an empty coffin and a fucked up excuse.

. . .

We had an issue getting Cleve to get in the car, however, due to the fact that he didn't want the cops involved, he obliged, along with his pregnant baby mama and *my* fiancée all wrapped in one. By the time we all climbed into the car and drove to my mom's house, Tony and I figured that the funeral home would soon realize my body had left the building during what they think was a robbery.

David ended up riding with Mary's dumb donkey butt to my mom's house in her car, so she wouldn't jump ship. As a matter of fact, I think I saw him pull up in the driver's seat, so scared Mary probably pissed in her pants the whole way here thinking his half drunk ass was going to wreck.

As I exited the car, my mom's home looked like heaven. I never thought that I would be this proud to see my mom again after being considered dead. I glance over at Cleve standing on the other side of the car. Shit. On two legs.

"Tony, take Cleve up the stairs so that Cleve can sit mom down before I come in." Glancing back at Cleve, I warn him again, "Try one thing, your whole shit is going up in smoke when I call the cops." I wave the cell in the air so his blind ass can see it.

He doesn't respond to me, that dear, sweet twin brother of mine. Fucking prick. I hope he trips up those mother fuckin' steps and busts his head on the bare brick. But then, that would traumatize my mom, so I need to scratch that idea. On top of that, I just got saved, so including that bloody brick thought, I have some work to do for my fucked up flesh. I will be sure to start after I set some shit off...get some of this shit off my chest while my heart still beats.

"Bring your ass here, Flee Flee." I glance down at her belly and then at her bare feet. "Country ass should have put on some damn shoes."

"Clive, I'm sorry."

"You damn right. Now shut the fuck up, hold my hand while we walk in, and if you even think to do some stupid shit, I'm breaking all these skinny ass fingers. Got it?"

She shakes her head, agreeing with me.

"And wipe those tears off your damn face before I give you something to cry about. Poke you in those bitches with a damn twig." Then I look her over once again. "Your stupid ass really slept with my brother."

She just stands there like an ass.

"Whose baby is it, Flee Flee?"

"I don't know, Clive."

"Aren't you one stupid woman?"

"You're supposed to be saved now, so where is the forgiveness, Clive, where?" she cries loudly, but I grab her cheeks and squeeze them tight.

"I'm supposed to be saved now, I know. But what the fuck about you, huh? Does killing my ass classify you as the one to remind someone about salvation or does it classify my hand to choke the shit out of you?" I let her face go, and her tears dry up fast. "You are the last person to talk about God to me or anger. God knows that in my brand new salvation, I'm doing the best I can because I didn't run your smelly ass over with this fucking car. You already tried to kill my ass with my brother, so don't think for one second

I'm going to prison or hell behind your sloppy, bummed out ass. To think I loved you, too."

She starts to walk, but I'm not even finished. I yank her butt back so she can hear what the heck I have to say before I go crazy as hell on both her and Cleve.

"And stop walking. Did I say walk yet?"

"No."

"See, you ass don't listen. Clean your ears the next time I say I love you so your stupid ass don't go and get with the next man, my brother," I stress, "who is jealous as hell of me! Now you got…man, I hope to God that baby in that belly isn't mine! I pray to God Almighty this baby isn't mine." I drop to my knees, underneath the tall oak tree to pray and make her fall down with me. "Pray!"

"About what?" she screams in terror and crying.

"Oh you don't know what to pray about? But your ass can scheme and scheme and scheme…" I feel a nudge on my shoulder in the middle of my insanity.

"Dude." It was David.

"What?"

"This looks pretty fucked up out here when you're supposed to be dead. Just in case the neighbors see you, try getting in the house fast."

I pop up. Forgot about that.

"Man, hide me," I say, grabbing his pant leg with my other hand.

"It's good, man, come on. They'll probably just think you're Cleve if they didn't already see him go in."

"Good," I stand up, look at Mary and call, "Looks like you might be going to jail today." Stupid ass hasn't said anything since she saw me at Tony's place. Shock I guess. It's either that or silence is the golden rule to keep her out of lock down. "Oh, by the way, what disease I catch? What did I have that took me out of here, Mary? Spreading false shit about me, but what about your maggoty asshole? What the hell did you put in my food? Or better yet, who the hell did you have come in to bang me upside my head after you doped me?"

"What!"

"Please don't act ignorant because you look ignorant enough. Let's go."

Entering the house slowly, I see my mom for the first time since being back to life. She's beautiful, and I can tell she has been crying all night because her eyes are puffy. Mom is still beautiful though.

When she lays eyes on me, I ease over to her because her mouth comes open but nothing comes out which petrified me because I didn't want to kill her dead on the spot. This whole surprise is a bit much, but wait until I drop the ball on this whole love triangle and killer square!

"Mom," I begin to speak while standing in the middle of the floor, Flee Flee beside me so she won't try to run and hide somewhere from this ball I'm about to drop.

"Clive? Baby?" Mom continues to stare at me, eyebrows down with that small wrinkle in the middle of them, because she is obviously digesting the sight of her dead son alive. "Oh Jesus, dear God!" Mom puts her hand on her heart, gets up, and walks over to me slowly. "Just like Lazarus, dear Jesus." She looks around at everyone. "My baby is alive!"

"It's me, mom, and yes, I'm alive." I stare right beside myself at Flee Flee to see if she has any type of joy in her eyes. None. This chick is scared straight, and I'm glad because her ass has absolutely no idea what I'm about to say next.

Mom comes and throws her arms around me, and I her, while keeping my hand tightly outside of Flee Flee's wrist. I glance over at Cleve as he leans on the wall with contempt drawn on his face. Tony appears as if he is in serious prayer with his eyes wide open.

David and Mary stroll inside, and to my surprise, Jonathan, Tommy and Auntie Bell come in behind them minutes later. The whole damn gang is here.

Releasing from my grasp, mom looks into my eyes. "How?"

I take a deep breath. "Sit down, ma." I turn to look back to Auntie Bell who has already started crying sitting on the chair behind me with her inhaler. Johnathan's mouth is gapped wide open as he reaches over to touch me as if I'm Jesus Christ or something while Tommy does absolutely nothing but stare. When my eyes meet his, Tommy looks away and to the floor.

That was weird as hell. I knew we weren't getting along but damn! I'm alive! As a matter of fact, from now on, people can call me Alive Clive!

"Well, everyone, I'm alive, and now that we have everyone here, I can tell you that I didn't even know what the hell happened to me...excuse me, ma. Sorry for the language," I state out of pure respect for the woman who brought me to this hell hole of a family that tried to send me there in a hand basket. "As I was saying, I'm out of the coffin now, but it wasn't until I heard what happened to me that I was able to put everything together. Isn't that funny?" I smiled the most devilish smile I could get. "Isn't it, Flee, I mean, Fee, baby?"

Felicia glances over at mom and then she turns to Cleve who won't even look at the women he probably got pregnant. After all this shit, I'm definitely not claiming the baby without a blood ass test. Sleeping with my brother and shit. Fucker and fuck her.

"Mom, turns out I'm not the butthole of the family after all. It's Cleve, mom. We are like a regular Cain and Abel. Remember that Biblical story all you sinners, huh?" I glance at mom, "Except you…and Aunt Bell." As I catch another look at Aunt Bell, she looks to be about to faint, so Jonathan rushed to hold her on the chair as she continues to gaze a me.

"Looks like at least four of you know already. I didn't just die, and it wasn't just someone who killed me randomly. This was planned, and it shows just how stupid the people are who planned this nonsense. It didn't work."

I drag Flee Flee along to stand next to Cleve, then I let her hand drop next to his. "Go ahead. Take Cleve's hand, and Cleve you take her hand because this stuff all started off with Cleve and Felicia whom I now reference as Flee Flee."

The phone rings in the kitchen.

"Don't answer it. It's probably just the funeral home about to go chaotic because they are just finding out that my body is missing," I joke. Really, this is honestly the funniest thing that has ever happened in all my life! Hilarious! I am actually a corpse on the run!

"Anyway, Cleve here decides that I am no good in his mind, turns my woman against me after showing her a lady that I slept with, thus, making his way into her heart. Flee gets mad at me with no questions asked and starts to pay me back by sleeping with Cleve. Guess what, everyone? Flee Flee is now pregnant with Cleve's baby – not mine!"

"This next part is was confuses the hell out of me though, Aunt Bell, Jonathan and Tommy," I state looking their way. "Cleve here decides to have Mary put something in my drink to knock me out. Why? Maybe so he can set me up or some crap, who knows, but if he wanted me out of the picture, Cleve could have just killed me himself. He claims, Mary," I turn to her, "that you were the one who decided on your own will to get someone to knock me the hell out, nearly killing me."

"No! No I didn't! Clive, I hate your ass, but I had nothing to do with you getting knocked upside your head. Cleve asked me to put something in your drink, yes! I did that, but it was because he wanted you to possibly get into a wreck on the way home and die! Ain't that right, Cleve? Tell him!"

Cleve's mouth was shut until mom reached up and slapped the fire out of it. This story hurt mom so much that she started to weep uncontrollably, but I kept going because this story was coming together nicely.

"Finally! Now this makes more sense! Cleve wanted me to wreck, kill myself, to have it look like an accident. So what? You mean to tell me that you didn't have a guy knock me over my head, Mary? Instead, you and Cleve planned to have me drive off a damn cliff?"

"Look…" she pauses, "I always wanted to get at you, truth be told, for hurting my cousin the way you did…"

"Not that again! How many times did I tell you that all we did is kiss? Your ugly cousin didn't have a chance with me, Mary! She's delusional!"

"That wasn't the only reason though, Clive. You were always to nasty to me! Just nasty! Don't you remember how you spit on the floor in my bar?"

"Yeah," I laugh. "And that was meant for you, but I missed."

"Well, I had to wipe that up! So yes! Yes, it was stuff like that why I decided to go with Cleve's idea to have you dead. Sure, I hoped you wrecked, but now that you're alive, I'm glad you are living." She crosses her arms and toots that big ass nose up in the air.

"Shut up!" I respond. "I heard you talk about how I died from some disease or some shit… excuse me mom. A woman glad I'm alive sure as hell wouldn't spread some crabs on my ass while I lay in my coffin."

"Well, I didn't land you in a coffin, Clive! Last time I saw you was getting hauled out of my bar, and I've been paranoid ever since. My fortune teller told me the dead would walk before I left the earth, and here you are."

"Well, she's a lie, too, because I wasn't even dead, dummy. I was drugged." Immediately, my thoughts on this fucked up story went to Cleve. "So Cleve, was it really you who sent someone in there to knock me out? Bust my ass upside my head, man?"

He didn't say a word, only shook his head. While he's doing that pitiful shit, I yell, "Did you?"

"No, man! No!" he yells back with his fists balled up like he could bust Flee Flee in her face because he damn sure wasn't going to hit me with his pussy ass. From behind maybe, but not man to man, face to face. He's always been a punk ass.

"So you guys mean to tell me some dude strolled into Mary's bar wanting my ass dead just as much as you two wanted me to suffer in death?"

Nobody answers. Tommy still has his hands in his pockets and his face looking at the floor, and that's odd to me. He should be one of the main ones in shock since he was one of the sad ones at my viewing. Something just wasn't right about him. He looks down each time hides something, like when we were little kids, and he hasn't changed that characteristic about his ass yet. So, I waltz over to him, and instead of him looking up, he continues to gaze at the floor while I stare at his dandruffy ass hair. He needs to wash that shit.

I whisper in his ear because at this particular point in my life, I am pretty well pissed. Being newly saved and this pissed isn't working well for me, therefore, I will hide the shit I'm about to say because it's about to sound insensitive as hell…plus I respect mom too much.

"Just what the fuck is wrong with your ass, Tommy?" I watch as the hairs in his ear flutter with what I know is my stink ass breath. It must be stink after all that sleeping in a coffin and nothing to eat or brush with.

Just then, I smell my cologne on this mug, and that's a first because he hates that shit. I turn to look at Jonathan, and he's just as dumbfounded as me while my poor Aunt Bell is probably still trying to figure out what is going on. She's such a good woman, just like mom, but I don't have time to hold her hand because the funeral is supposed to happen soon. I suspect a knock at the door any time now with the fucked up news that I'm alive. Well, fucked up for them. Fucking great for my warm blooded ass.

"Aren't you happy to see me?" I whisper again. Still, no answer from Tommy's mouth, but he does try to walk away from me. "Oh what? You have some sort of chip on your shoulder still about that old mess? Man, I'm alive. I have the prize money and more in my house…"

Wait a minute. I know this mother fucker didn't… Before I said anything else, I shove Tommy up against the wall, and his brother comes running.

"Clive, man, what are you doing? Get off my brother, man!"

"Man, sit the fuck down! Tommy's been in my house, and he knows it!"

"What are you talking about, Clive? Let him go!" Jonathan yells, pulling me by my neck from behind, so I let him go only to slam Jonathan on the floor beneath my foot. I pressed hard on his chest, and he gives in by tapping out.

I turn my attention back to Tommy who hasn't moved his punk ass yet. "What the fuck were you doing in my house, Tommy. Flee gets me that cologne, and I don't even know where she gets it from."

Silence. I start to look him over really good.

"You sure are clean, Tommy." I smile. "Got new rags on and shit. Isn't he clean, y'all?" I ask the rest of the family who are now looking at me like I'm the trouble maker. Then, I turn my attention back to Tommy. "Where'd you get the money to get such nice clothes, cousin? You know something? I bet you got the money from my house, didn't you, Tommy?"

Nothing. No words at all come from his mouth, but this time, he stares straight in my face.

"Do you know I was going to give you that money that I won, Tommy, since you're such a sore loser? Yeah, I was going to give you all of it, but I bet you went into my stash too, didn't you, and took all the money, not just the winnings from the art show? When, Tommy? When did you take it?"

"I needed that money!" Tommy hollers in rage that I've never seen is weak ass in before. "I lost my condo because you cheated me! You cheated me! Man, you ain't shit! I entered that contest with the best I could do because I knew I needed the money," he continues as he looks around the room at everyone, "and I also knew that I could win!"

"I offered you a room in my pad, Tommy. You decided to move in with Aunt Bell."

"I went in debt, and all you did was walk by me like you could care less. That was my prize money. So, yeah, I took it right out of your house after finding out your win was rigged. Fuck you! Go ahead and hit me! But I took what was rightfully mine, Clive."

As he talks, I simply stare at him quietly until I figure more of this shit out. Things are coming together in my head by assumption, but my ass won't be made an ass of today.

"Mary, do you know where Candice lives?"

"Candice?"

"Yeah, crazy ass Candice!"

"Yes. Yes, I know. Why?"

"David, go with Mary to go get her. How far away is she?"

"You know what, fuck you, Clive!" yells Tommy.

"Fuck me? What makes you so irritated at the fact that Candice is coming? Old crack head Candice that doesn't know shit but how to get money to get high. Wait a minute! Well, look at this shit!" I pull the unread note out of my pocket. "I forgot to read the damn note she left in my hand. Can you believe the chick can write, Tommy?"

I hold the note up really high in the air. I can't believe I was so hooked on beating the hell out of Cleve, Flee

Flee and escaping my funeral that I forgot to even read the damn letter! Honestly, I didn't think the shit to be that important when I heard her say she didn't know who it was that hit me. I just thought that it was a stupid ass apology letter, but now, this shit is coming together.

"Don't just sit there everyone, gather around," I announce while Tommy glares like he's about to hit me in the throat. Despite his whimpy ass threatening stance, no one is threatened because they know he's a joke, so they all gather around, including the suspected killers to listen as I read the note. Tommy has nowhere to go. Why? Because everyone has him stuck in the corner incidentally to hear me read.

"Dear Clive, I know you're dead now, but I believe in spirits being right

here with us. I also know that I'm on drugs, and you don't take me seriously most of the time you see me. We don't really know each other besides outside Mary's store where we see each other, but I kind of wanted you to know that I took some money from someone named Tommy who told me to get someone to knock you off. The reason I know his name is because he answered his cell phone on speaker by accident when he was walking away, and I heard his name – Tommy. Well, anyway, I just walked around a bit and found someone who needed a hit bad, told them to go inside the bar and off you. Since I'd just seen you and what you were wearing, I showed him the money, and when I told him to go into the bar, I knew that he would find you there. Thing is, I just didn't know that he would kill you for real, so I want to apologize for sending a complete stranger to me inside the bar because I really didn't know that he would do you any harm. I can't go to the cops about it because I was too stoned to care about what he looked like, but I do know that I was the one who told him you were in there. Sorry, Clive, but I just wanted to get high. Love you. Miss you. Candice."

I fold the letter and place it back into my pocket. Tommy. Good old Tommy was in on my killing, too!

"Do you hear that, mom? Cleve, Flee Flee, Mary, Tommy and old drug head Candice all tried to off me at the same time and fucking failed! Pussy asses!" I look around in a fit of laughter, and continue my rant on Tommy. "Unball your damn fists because you aren't about to do shit to me. I bet that money you gave to Candice was some of my damn money, now wasn't it? Y'all hear this shit, right? Make sure I'm not really dead and dreaming and shit…excuse me for my language again, ma."

Mom simply nods her head, seemingly unbothered by my cussing. She even looks like she wants to join me! Shoot, I have a damn right to be pissed off, and everyone in this room knew it.

"Well, we have an empty coffin ready to go into the ground, Tommy. You want it?"

Angrily he responds, "You ain't doing shit to me! Candice is a liar!"

"She might be high, but a liar she isn't. At least not by this letter she isn't. This shit is too hard to believe, I mean really! This type of fucked up shit only happens in the damn movies or a fucking book, and my ass isn't in either. This is real fucking life, but question is, Tommy, how the hell did you do it?"

"Did you really try to kill Clive, baby?" Aunt Bell asked heartbroken. These are the first words that she's said since she saw me.

"Ma," Tommy states, "It's not like what you think. It all happened so fast, ma."

"Lord Jesus, my child!"

"See what you did, Tommy? Now look, here's the deal. I won't call the law, if you spill the fuckin' beans, man. How about that?"

Tommy looks at me hard as hell. I know he won't jump in my face while I'm right here to deck his ass out, so all he can do is take the deal. Just like everyone else, I wait for him to start with his version of events that led to my death.

"Clive," Tommy states.

I look around dumbfounded just to get under his skin even more. "You addressing me, Tommy?" Of course, I know he's addressing me, but he's talking a bit too softly. His murdering ass needs to speak up.

"You stole from me. I lost everything I ever wanted behind you and your games, man. I was laughed at, and everyday inside of myself, I knew that I was the better artist. I deserved all the acclaim that you got on the streets. It was me who deserved to make a living doing what I loved, not work at a grocery store all night, cleaning floors. So yeah, I took your money. I found it one day last week when I broke in to ruin one of your paintings. You'd left it open, your whole stash was left uncovered underneath the floor."

"Oh really?"

"Yeah, really," he responds. "I was friends with a doctor who I knew owed me a big favor long before he became a physician. So when I found Candice, and she got some dude to off you, I had it arranged that he would get you that night. I paid him and everything. Thing is that I didn't know he would lie and pronounce you dead, slow your heart down with some drug, and take my money."

"Your money? You mean, my money. My life savings, Tommy!"

"Hell no! None of that shit was yours. I was owed that for taking all your shit over the years. Always being the underdog." He goes silent, and then speaks again. "I wanted you dead," he says deeply. "I dream of your death, but I guess that hasn't come true. I even knew of your quick to bury me will, so I knew that if the morticians would get you in the ground fast enough…"

"I ought to kill you myself, Tommy," Ma says from the

background. "I trusted you with my son, and you knew that he may not have been dead."

"Ma, what happened?" Suddenly, I got confused. Trusted him with me? What did Tommy have to do with my burial?

"I got sick, Clive, after I heard you were gone. I mean, I thought you were dead, so I really got sick, and told ma to let Tommy handle the arrangements at the funeral home," Cleve interjects.

"And that's when I hit you in the head again. Plus, I asked the mortician if I could wrap you really good and tight. When he said yes, I did. Problem was that he said everything but your head, so I left that uncovered. See where that got me. You're alive."

I stare Tommy over. "You're a real bitch ass dude." Then, I take my hand and smack the shit out of him.

Then I continue to smack his crooked ass four more times until Jonathan stops me.

The phone begins to ring off the hook, but no one dare answers it. We all know who it is. The funeral home. Who else is going to call off the hook on the day of my burial at my mom's house. Everyone who loves me is right here. My bad, half of the people who love me are in this house with me. The other half are hellyuns who wanted to toast to my damn death. Good thing I didn't put cremation in my will.

"Well, shit, Mary! Your ass ain't as bad as I took you for! You're fucking worse! And Cleve, you still ain't worth the shit you step in with your fuckin' non-hourglass girl you stole from me. Tony, can you lead us all in a moment of prayer, please. I think old Tommy here needs to be saved before I kill him."

"Clive, look. I can call the cops right now, and handle this. Let him go."

"Call the cops? I'm saved, right, Tony? I'm a man of my word. I told this man that I wouldn't lock him up, so the only other thing left to do is kill him," I spin around to face everyone, "Or let him go free. Which one is it?" I turn to look at Tommy. "Which one, Tommy?"

In the background, the sounds of both ma and auntie are piercing my ears as they wail over me and Tommy. Surely, they were thinking about how much they love us both, but one of us went bad. To ma, it was Tommy. To auntie, it was me. To me, I didn't give a fuck at this point. I just want to murder his ass like he tried to bury me in warm blood.

"Some cars are pulling up, Clive."

"What cars, Tony?" I ask, looking back at Tony.

Before he could even answer, I feel metal slam up against my left temple.

"Breathe wrong, and I'll kill you. Now I'm about to get out of here with the rest of the money I have at the house, and you're going to tell the cops and the funeral home that there was a big mistake. You got it?"

"What the fuck you got this gun at my head for, Tommy? You don't have the mother fuckin' guts to pull that bitch trigger on me. You're so pathetic that you got a damn drug addict to do your dirty work for you, so you can lower your damn water gun from my head!"

"Stand down, Clive," Cleve warns. "I think he's serious, bro. Stand down."

I turn all the way around, allowing the pistol to rub the very back of my head as I face everyone in the living room. "Shut the fuck up, Cleve. If you would, you would pull the trigger before this bone ass head behind me. Aunt Bell, do you see your son? Is this the chicken shit you raised? Ma, is he serious? This fool wouldn't shoot me if his own life depended on it."

The doorbell rings, but when it rings, absolutely no one goes to answer it.

"Well! Somebody besides ma get the door. I told you this pussy won't pull a damn trigger. Answer the fucking door so this bitch can take his ass to jail!"

As Jonathan goes to open the door, I can see through the window that it's the funeral director and the authorities following a ways behind.

"Ha ha! Well," I chuckle as I turn back to face Tommy and the water gun,

"It looks like I didn't have to call the cops like I..."

In the middle of my damn sentence, the gun goes off. This mother fucker shot my ass right between the fucking eyes right as the funeral director was telling Jonathan the last damn thing I hear …

"…we need the body…"

Jesus, forgive me. I'm dead.

THE END

Preview <u>Execution's Karma</u>

Year 2499

"Kill him!" shouts the crowd of people inside the stadium who paid big money to celebrate the witnessing of the latest execution. The streets are packed full of babies, children and parents gone wild at the projection plastered on the cement stadium walls that show the inside of the dome where the execution is to take place. Some of the children are crying while their parents coerce them into believing that executions are just and fair, used to teach lessons that you don't live to tell about. There are other children who have already learned to behave as their parents, thriving off of watching someone die the death.

For those who can't travel to the stadium to watch the execution, there is complete online access to the killing while otherwise it's televised on what is known as Channel End which is a life saver for those at work during the execution. They can simply look up and watch.

Death. The people believe it's the answer to every problem, and the governor gives his stamp of approval. It's taken over two hundred years to get citizens of the United States of America to the place where they don't care about bloodshed and screams of mercy while someone is begging to live just for the sake of being. For the most part, society now has no shock when they see death, and they even laugh when people cry.

It's called desensitization of the colonies, and it's a plan the government has had for centuries that has finally taken root. People, many of them, simply don't care anymore about life. With no root for their own existence, they've learned to kill and be killed. The only thing that stops most of them from killing and not breaking the law is being executed at the stadium because ironically, they tend to still have love for themselves which is typically a quite ignorant way of thinking. Yet, it's true for this bunch. This is why in today's society, families keep their children near and strangers far. There is no natural affection left inside most of the people, and mercy isn't an option. It's the way of not just a free society, but a free feeling society, ruled by pure raw emotion that's created by the constant infliction of visual pain. Watching someone die has become an object of affection, and no other form of entertainment exists anymore.

It's convict number three hundred who is due to see his own destruction, and the number is marked clearly on his forehead for the number of times this type of execution has drawn record numbers of onlookers. Vendors are selling their most popular foods named after the type of killing for this week – shocking strawberry, laid out lemonade, and burning rubber hot dogs are to name a few. It's rather sick to drink a beverage or swallow down food named after a lynching, or in more politically correct terms, an execution, but people fill their guts anyway.

Execution convict number three hundred has only been on lock down for seventy-two hours total. He was arrested for killing a store clerk in cold blood, and now people are hungry to watch the finale of this killer's life. Governor Dearth is just as hungry. As a matter of fact, he's starving, which is why he's starting the execution minutes early. While holding his arms up high into the air as if he's feeding off of the souls of the non-saints, ain'ts and the rest, he speaks into the microphone.

"Good evening, and welcome to EX-300!" he yells, amped while raising his beloved twenty-seven year old son's hand in the air along with his. Robert Dearth is his son's name, by the way, and he's in training to become the next governor of the newest state in what's left of the union named South Texas due to its split resulting from a nasty civil war. Robert Dearth, if his dad has something to do with it, will be the next governor for a long time. Like father like son goes the saying, so there should be absolutely no problem with Robert garnering the votes because not only does the public adore Governor Sam Dearth, the last two presidents seem to take his word as law.

"This is all about crime, ladies, gentleman and children, and this man that we see beneath all of us is a stone cold, hardened criminal with no chance of redemption. He has murdered," he pauses to emphasize the word murdered, "a clerk in a store who did nothing to deserve it, but now," he says, increasing the volume of his voice, "he will get what he deserves when the electricity races through his body, making him lifeless just like the clerk he took off the earth when he shed innocent blood! Let's hear it!"

"Kill him! Kill him!" shouts the crowd over and over again while Robert Dearth smiles, amazed by all the followers his father has managed to influence. Governor Sam Dearth smiles back at the sight of his son being a man with the ability to harden his heart when necessary because one would need that quality in order to execute without all the nightmares that follow.

Akirim Press Books
Books by Mirika Mayo Cornelius

(mirikacornelius.com)

Secret

Colored Lily: Poppa Took My Innocence

Paton

Curse the Cotton

Ain't Quite What I Thought!

Ain't Quite What I Thought! 2

Inside the Gates of Doons

Murders at Gabriel's Trails: The Complete 5 Part Series with bonus Sins of Bain

Deception at Gabriel's Trails: The Complete Series

Sins of Bain: The Extended Version

Sunny Sides of My Shade

First Degree Sins

Cold Blooded Goons

I Thought I Was Alone

Most Wanted Felon

Disguised by a Raging Smile

Books by Rod Cornelius

(rodcornelius.com)

Diggin' Gold

The Trusted

Single Again

Ghetto Eyes

The Best Kept Secrets

Ugly

He Beats Me

Love, Lies & Lipstick

Books by Cyan Deane

(mirikacornelius.com/cyan-deane)

Dead Man's Mayhem

Execution's Karma